SOPHIE HITS SIX

Beano sat in the doorway wiffling his nose madly.

SOPHIE
HITS SIX

DICK KING-SMITH

illustrated by
DAVID PARKINS

CANDLEWICK PRESS
CAMBRIDGE, MASSACHUSETTS

Text copyright © 1991 by Fox Busters Ltd.
Illustrations copyright © 1991 by David Parkins

First U.S. paperback edition 1995

Library of Congress Cataloging-in-Publication Data

King-Smith, Dick.
Sophie hits six/Dick King-Smith; illustrated by David Parkins.—
1st U.S. ed.
Summary: The year that Sophie turns six, she sees her cat give birth
to kittens, gets a pet rabbit from her Aunt Al, and pursues her dream
of acquiring a dog. Sequel to "Sophie's Snail" and "Sophie's Tom."
ISBN 1-56402-216-1 (hardcover)—1-56402-462-8 (paperback)
[1. Pets—Fiction.]   I. Parkins, David, ill.   II. Title.
PZ7.K616So   1993   92-54692
[Fic]—dc20

2 4 6 8 10 9 7 5 3 1

Printed in Great Britain

The pictures in this book were done in pen and ink.

Candlewick Press
2067 Massachusetts Avenue
Cambridge, Massachusetts 02140

CONTENTS

"One thing's certain," said Sophie's father. "You can't call him ... her ... Tom anymore."

"One thing's certain," said Sophie's father. "You can't call him . . . her . . . Tom anymore."

Tom was Sophie's black cat, who had come from nowhere and adopted her and had now, much to everyone's surprise, given birth to four kittens.

"Female cats are called queens," said Sophie's mother. "You could call her Queenie."

"I don't like that," said Sophie.

"How about Elizabeth?" said Matthew, who was eight, two and a half years older than Sophie and ten minutes older than his twin brother Mark.

"Why Elizabeth?"

"Well, it's the Queen's name."

"Or Diana?" said Mark.

"Why?"

"That's what the Princess of Wales is named. She'll be queen one day."

"I can't wait that long to give my cat another name," said Sophie.

The twins, however, were quite taken with this idea of royalty. As often happened, they had the same thought at the same moment, and they looked at one another and grinned and said, "How about Fergie?"

"Spelled F-U-R-gie," said Sophie's father, and everyone laughed, except Sophie.

"You're all silly, stupid, and sickening!" she said, and she stomped off, hands shoved deep into the pockets of her old jeans, a frown of disapproval on her round face.

She plodded up to the attic at the top of the house, where all the animals of her toy farm were laid out. Here, in the depths of an old armchair, lay her cat, nursing the four kittens, one tabby, one tortoiseshell, one black with a white bib and white feet, and one exactly like its mother, whose black coat Sophie now stroked.

"I can't call you Tom anymore," she said, "because you're not one, are you, my dear?"

"Nee-o," said the cat, or that's how it sounded to Sophie.

"I suppose I could call you Thomasina, but I don't really like that, do you?"

"Neoo-o."

"Mom and Daddy and the twins weren't any help."

Sophie rubbed the tip of her nose, a sure sign that she was thinking deeply.

"I wish Aunt Al was here," she said. "I bet she'd have a good idea."

*Sophie sat on the arm of the old chair,
stroking her nameless cat.*

Aunt Al was Sophie's father's great-aunt, and therefore Sophie's great-great-aunt. When she had first been told this, she had imagined Aunt Al as enormous, but actually she was very small, with thin legs like a bird. She was nearly eighty-two years old, and she lived in the Highlands of Scotland. She and Sophie had become good friends.

Sophie sat on the arm of the old chair, stroking her nameless cat and wondering whether to write a letter to Aunt Al.

"The trouble is," she said, "I'd have to have help with the spelling and everything, and anyway it would all take a long time."

Just then she heard the ring of the telephone downstairs, and she jumped up, grinning.

"Yikes!" said Sophie. "That's it! I'll call her!"

Something told Sophie it might be best to say nothing to the others about this phone call. It might be very expensive to telephone the Highlands because they were so high. If they ask me, she thought, I'll tell them I did it (for Sophie didn't approve of lying), but if they don't know, they won't ask.

So she waited that afternoon, a fine Saturday afternoon in early May, until her brothers had gone off to play football (which they never got tired of) with some friends, her mother had gone to do some shopping, and her father was working in the garden.

Sophie found Aunt Al's number in the phone book and carefully dialed it. She heard the ring and then Aunt Al's brisk voice, as loud and clear as if she were in the room, saying, "Hello. Who is it?"

"It's Sophie."

"Sophie? My niece?"

"Great-great-niece, Aunt Al."

"Great-great-aunt to you. How nice to hear

Sophie found Aunt Al's number in the
phone book and carefully dialed it.

your voice, Sophie. Are you okay? Anything the matter?"

"Yes, there is."

"Nobody ill or anything?"

"No. It's my cat."

"Tom?"

"Yes. Well, no. You see, it's not Tom anymore, because she's had four babies."

"Whew!" said Aunt Al. "Surprise, surprise."

"And so she's got to have a new name," said Sophie, "and I can't think of a good one. That's why I'm calling you, to ask if you can help me."

"Right," said Aunt Al. "Give me a minute."

Sophie waited, imagining, as she always did, Aunt Al sitting on top of a mountain somewhere, surrounded by golden eagles and blue hares and red deer. In a minute her voice would come whizzing down the telephone wires, down the mountainside, off the edge of the Highlands, out of Scotland, and almost all

14

the way to the bottom of England, all in a fraction of a second.

"Tomboy," said Aunt Al.

"What?" said Sophie. "That's even worse than plain Tom."

"No, it's not. Do you know what a tomboy is?"

"No."

"A tomboy is a high-spirited girl who likes romping around. Your cat's high-spirited, isn't she?"

"Yes."

"Well then."

One of the reasons why Sophie and Aunt Al got along so well was that they were both direct, no-nonsense people. They did what had to be done, said what had to be said, and that was the end of it.

"Okay," said Sophie. "Thanks. See you."

"Sometime in the summer, I hope," said Aunt Al, and hung up.

* * *

At dinnertime Sophie said, "My cat's got her new name."

"What is it?" chorused the twins.

"Tomboy."

"What?" they said. "That's even worse than plain Tom."

"Don't they teach you anything in your class?" said Sophie scornfully. "You're ingerant, that's what you are."

"Don't you meant 'ignorant'?" said her father.

"That too," said Sophie.

"But Sophie," said her mother, "do you know what 'tomboy' means?"

"Of course," said Sophie. "A tomboy is a high-spirited girl who likes romping around. Can I get up please?"

"Yes," said her mother, "if you've finished.

"Don't they teach you anything in
your class?" said Sophie scornfully.

Where are you off to?"

"To feed Tomboy," said Sophie, "and to find names for my four kittens." And off she plodded.

Sophie, though small, was very determined, and a worrying thought crossed her mother's mind.

"I hope," she said, "she doesn't think that she can keep those kittens."

"One thing's certain," said Sophie's father, "she can't. As soon as they're old enough, we must find them homes. One cat's enough, let alone five."

Up in the attic, Sophie addressed the kittens. Her firm ambition in life was to be a lady farmer, and she knew well that farmers, whether ladies or not, were always looking to increase their flocks and herds.

"Now, my dears," she said, "let's hope that you're all girls. Then, once you're big enough, you can all have babies too. And suppose each of you has four, that will make . . . let's see — " and Sophie began to count on her fingers.

"Sophie takes a lot of trouble with her work,"
said the teacher.

DOWN ON THE FARM

Sophie liked school. Learning things, she had decided by the end of her first term, was interesting, even though they did not have farming lessons, as she had hoped they would. But she could see that to be a lady farmer one day meant that you had to know how to read and write and do arithmetic, so she set about these tasks in her usual determined manner.

Early in the spring term, her teacher was asked by the headmistress, "How is Sophie getting along?"

"Very well really. She takes a lot of trouble with her work. She tells me she wants to be a farmer, so we do a lot of math with the bottles of milk in the morning! Strange little girl though — lives in a world of her own."

"Still a bit of a loner, is she?"

"A bit. She certainly doesn't have a special friend in the class."

"Who's your special friend, Sophie?" her mother said one evening.

"Tomboy," said Sophie.

"No, I mean at school. In your class."

"Dawn?" asked Matthew.

Dawn was a pretty little fair-haired girl, always beautifully dressed, the exact opposite of Sophie, both in looks and nature.

"Yuck!" said Sophie.

"Duncan?" said Mark.

Duncan was a very small, fat, short-legged boy with red hair. A onetime playmate of Sophie's, he had been "stolen" by Dawn while Sophie was out sick with chicken pox. Both had paid dearly for this.

"He's stupid," said Sophie.

"Don't you like any of the children in your class, Sophie?" asked her father.

"Not really. Andrew's all right."

Her mother waited until Sophie had plodded off upstairs to play with the kittens, and then she said to the twins, "Who's Andrew?"

"He's new this term," said Mark.

"He's a farmer's son," said Matthew.

"Aha! Is he nice?"

"Dunno," they said. "We don't play with the little kids."

In fact, Sophie hadn't decided whether Andrew was nice or not — nor did she care. Once she had found out that his father was a farmer, she had decided to make friends with him. Then, she thought, he would invite her to the farm, and after a while she would be able to go there often. She would make sure she was so useful to Andrew's father that he would ask her to come and help regularly — every day perhaps. And then, when she left school, she could work there. And, later, she and Andrew would probably get married and have four babies, just like Tomboy, and live happily ever after on the farm.

With such a prospect in view, what did it matter whether she liked Andrew or not?

Sophie took her time. She did not try to bribe him with sweets, as Dawn would have done, nor did she set out to boss him as she had bossed Duncan. Instead she began to ask Andrew lots of questions — about farming of course — whenever she just happened to find herself standing next to him in the playground.

Sophie's reason for this questioning was purely and simply to learn things that would be useful to her one day.

Andrew, however, a sturdy little boy of about the same height and build as Sophie, but with very fair, almost white hair, was flattered to be thought so knowledgeable, and answered these queries readily, if not always accurately.

"Your dad's a farmer, isn't he?" was Sophie's first question.

"Yes," said Andrew.

"I'm going to be a farmer when I grow up."

"You can't."

"Why not?"

"Farmers are men."

"Well," said Sophie, "I'm going to be a lady farmer. So there."

"I'm going to be a man farmer."

"You're lucky," said Sophie, "living on a farm now. Does your dad have cows?"

"Yes, hundreds."

Andrew set off around the playground shouting,
"Broom-a-broom-a-broom-a-broom!"

"Can you milk them?"

"Yes, 'course I can."

"What else can you do?"

"Drive a tractor," said Andrew. He gripped an imaginary steering wheel, engaged an imaginary gear, and set off around the playground shouting, *"Broom-a-broom-a-broom-a-broom!"*

Sophie stood waiting until he had completed a circuit, pulled on an imaginary hand brake, and switched it off.

"I wish I could see your tractor," she said.

But instead of the hoped-for invitation, Andrew only said, "It's green."

"How much did it cost?"

"'Bout half a million pounds."

"Yikes!" said Sophie. "Your dad must be rich!"

"He is," said Andrew. "And I'm going to be too when I grow up. I shall have six tractors and I shall have cows and pigs and sheep and chickens and ducks and geese and . . ."

". . . a Shetland pony?" said Sophie.

"Lots of them."

Each day now, at morning and afternoon recess, Sophie plied Andrew with questions of an agricultural nature. The fact that she monopolized his company did not escape the notice of her brothers.

Matthew and Mark prided themselves on being fast runners and, with the school's field day in mind, spent their time in high-speed dashes across the playground — in which, not surprisingly, they almost always tied. However, they could not help but see that each time they hurled themselves against the chain link fence that acted as a finish line, there were Sophie and Andrew, dark and fair heads together, chattering away nonstop.

"Sophie's always talking to that Andrew," they said to their parents.

"Why shouldn't she?" said their mother "It's nice she's made a special friend at last, and he's a nice-looking little boy too."

"He's not my special friend," said Sophie. "He just knows all about farming, that's all."

"Must be a clever chap," said her father. "How old is he?"

"Five."

"Imagine!"

"Sophie likes Andrew!" chanted the twins, and they ran off before Sophie had time to tell them that not only were they silly, but also both stupid and sickening.

"Don't take any notice, darling," said her mother. "They're only teasing."

"It doesn't bother me," said Sophie loftily. "They only do it to be iterating."

"I'm not having those kittens making a mess
all over the attic," said Sophie's mother.

"Don't you mean 'irritating'?" said her father.

"Both," said Sophie.

A couple of weeks went by, during which time Sophie continued her questioning of Andrew. She was also made to move her own livestock from the attic to the potting shed at the end of the garden.

"I'm not having those kittens making a mess all over the attic," her mother said.

"But they'll make a mess all over the potting shed," said Sophie.

"And you'll clean it all up. That's what farmers spend most of their time doing, you know — cleaning up all the muck their animals make."

"Your cows must make an awful lot of

*At the end of the school day Andrew's
mother saw her son approaching.*

cowpats," Sophie said to Andrew the next day. "I wish I could see them."

"See the cowpats?"

"No, the cows."

"You can if you like."

"You'll have to ask me over."

"All right."

Sophie sighed. Silly boy, she thought, I'll have to fix it all myself, I can see.

"You ask your mommy to ask my mommy if it's okay," she said, "and then she can bring me."

"All right."

So at the end of the school day Andrew's mother saw her son approaching, his hand firmly held by a stocky little girl with an untidy mop of dark hair and a determined expression.

Sophie's mother arrived in time to hear the ensuing conversation.

"Go on, Andrew, ask her," said Sophie.

"Mom," said Andrew. "Can Sophie come over?"

"She'd obviously fixed the whole thing up herself," Sophie's mother said to her husband. "I'd never even met the boy's mother before, but she seemed very nice. I said we'd pick Sophie up again about six."

"She'll have gotten herself into a big mess, I'm sure."

"Oh, I don't know — I made her take her boots."

The phone rang in the hall.

Sophie's mother came back from answering it.

"You were right," she said. "That was Andrew's mother saying could I bring some clean clothes, Sophie is absolutely filthy. She slipped and sat down in a really squelchy cowpat."

"Ah, well," said Sophie's father. "Farming's just like any other job. Start at the bottom and work up."

*Sophie decided to call the kittens
Molly, Dolly, Holly, and Polly.*

BEANO

Down in the potting shed the four kittens were growing fast. Though Sophie kept the door shut while she was at school (for fear that a fierce cat-eating dog might jump into the garden and gobble them all up), there was a small hole in the boards at the back of the shed, through which Tomboy came and went at her pleasure.

Sophie liked choosing names, and, confident that the kittens were all female, had decided after much thought to call them Molly, Dolly, Holly, and Polly.

"Those are all girls' names," her father said.

"They're all girls," said Sophie.

"How do you know?"

"I just do."

"Wouldn't it be better to give them names that sound different?" her mother asked. "Those all sound the same."

"It's easy to tell them apart," Sophie said. "Molly's the tabby, Dolly's the tortoiseshell, Holly's the black-and-white one, and Polly's all black."

Her mother sighed. "That's not quite what I meant," she said.

"It makes no difference," said Sophie's father. "In a couple of weeks they'll all have to go, Sophie. I hope you realize that?"

"Can't I even keep one?"

"No."

"It's not fair," said Sophie to the twins. "They won't let me keep any of the kittens."

"You've got Tomboy," said Matthew.

38

"You don't want five cats," said Mark.

"I do," said Sophie. "While I'm waiting to be a lady farmer I could be a lady cat-breeder. If I could keep Molly and Dolly and Holly and Polly and they all had babies, I could sell loads of kittens and save up loads of money for my farm." And she pointed at her piggy bank, on whose side was stuck a note that read:

FARM MUNNY
THANK YOU
SOPHIE

"They won't let you," said the twins.

Two weeks went by, and Sophie's father placed an advertisement in the local paper.

"Four pretty kittens," it said. "Good homes wanted."

"I wouldn't mind, if only you were boys,"

*"Was it a boy you wanted, or a girl?" Sophie's mother
asked the large, tall lady.*

said Sophie as she sat on the floor of the potting shed while the kittens played around her. "But it's such a waste. Female animals are definitely the most important — any farmer knows that."

Just then she heard voices, and in a moment her mother appeared in the doorway with a large, tall lady.

"Ah," she said. "Here's Sophie, with her kittens. Now, was it a boy you wanted, or a girl?"

"A queen," said the large, tall lady. "A female."

"These are all female, Sophie says. Can you tell?"

"Of course," said the large, tall lady. "Kept cats all my life. One of these is certainly a little queen, I can tell you that straight off," and she pointed at Dolly.

"How do you know?" said Sophie's mother.

"Tortoiseshell. Torts are always female. Let's

have a look at the other three ... let's see now ... you're a boy ... and you're a boy ... and you're a boy. Three little toms."

"Oh," said Sophie glumly.

"So I'll take the little tortoiseshell if I may. Does she have a name?"

"Dolly," said Sophie gloomily.

"And you're Sophie?"

Sophie nodded. Only one female, she thought, and she has to go and pick that one.

"So how much do you want for Dolly, Sophie?" asked the large, tall lady.

"Excuse me," said Sophie's mother. "I can hear the phone ringing. I won't be a minute," and out she went.

Sophie rubbed the tip of her nose. I'll say a silly price, she thought, and then she'll say, "Oh, that's much too much," and then she won't take Dolly.

"Five pounds," she said.

The large, tall lady produced her purse, and from it she took a five pound note.

"That's fair enough," she said. "I don't believe in getting something for nothing," and she handed Sophie the money.

"And when the woman had gone off with the kitten," Sophie's mother said to her husband that evening, "I went down to the potting shed to comfort Sophie, and, lo and behold, she'd made five pounds."

"'Farm Munny'!" said Sophie's father admiringly. "And still three to go!"

However Sophie was to find that other people were not so generous.

In the days that followed, the black-and-white kitten went to an old man who gave Sophie ten pence ("For your piggy bank, young lady"), and the tabby to a jolly couple who gave Sophie a nice smile and a pat on the head.

The tabby went to a jolly couple who gave Sophie a smile and a pat on the head.

Now only the black kitten remained.

"I wonder where you will go, my dear?" said Sophie sadly. Soon there would be no kittens to play with.

"You'll miss them, won't you?" said Sophie to Tomboy.

"Nee-o."

Just then Sophie heard her mother calling.

"Hurry!" she cried. "It's Aunt Al on the phone. She wants to talk to you."

Sophie galloped up the lawn.

"Hello, Aunt Al," she said breathlessly.

"You sound winded."

"I was running."

"Tomboy's kittens. Are they all gone?"

"All but one."

"Keep it for me."

"For you?"

"Yes. My old cat died. He was very ancient, miles older than me if you multiply by seven

45

like you do with a dog's age. Daddy's coming up to Scotland on business next month and bringing me back to visit. Do you think you could keep your last kitten another four weeks, till I can collect it?"

"Oh yes!"

"What color is it?"

"Black, like Tomboy."

"Lucky," said Aunt Al.

"If they come up to you from the right-hand side."

"What's its name?"

"Polly."

"So it's female?"

"No, actually. I thought she was but he isn't."

"We'll have to change the name. So he gets used to a new one before I come."

"You choose then," said Sophie.

"Right," said Aunt Al. "Give me a minute."

Sophie waited, thinking of Aunt Al on her mountain and feeling very glad that the black kitten would live happily at the top of the Highlands.

"Are you still there?" asked Aunt Al.

"Yes."

"Ollie. Short for Oliver."

"Okay."

"How much do you want for him?"

"Nothing."

"We'll see about that."

They sounded equally determined.

"Let me speak to your mother."

"Okay," said Sophie. "Here she is. See you," and she plodded off down to the potting shed to tell the good news to Tomboy and Ollie.

Meanwhile her mother was saying on the telephone, "In exchange for the kitten, you mean? What a nice idea, Aunt Al — you know how crazy about animals she is . . . no, her

Sophie made sure Ollie came up to Aunt Al from the right-hand side.

father won't object, I'll make sure of that . . .
yes, we'll see about somewhere to keep it . . .
no, we'll keep it a secret, won't say a word —
you can spring the surprise when you come."

When Aunt Al did come, four weeks later, the
very first thing she wanted to do was to see
Ollie. And Sophie made sure that he came up
to her from the right-hand side.

"He's beautiful," said Aunt Al, picking the
kitten up, while Tomboy wrapped herself
around the old lady's thin bird's legs and made
her steam-engine noise. "He's the spitting
image of his mother. You'll miss him, won't
you, Tomboy?"

"Nee-o."

"It's very nice of you to give him to me,
Sophie," said Aunt Al. "Maybe I can give you
something in return, one of these days."

*   *   *

49

Little did Sophie know, when she went to bed that night, what was covered over with an old sheet at the back of the garage.

Little did she guess, when she woke the next morning, what would be put in the potting shed while she was at school, and while her great-great-aunt was paying a visit to the local pet shop.

Little did she dream that, when she came home that afternoon, Aunt Al would suggest a walk down to the potting shed and then, before they went in, would say to her, "Shut your eyes, Sophie."

"Why?"

"Surprise."

Sophie shut her eyes and felt her hand held by another that was skinny and bony and curled like a bird's claws.

"Okay," said Aunt Al. "You can look now."

There, sitting placidly in a large new rabbit

hutch, was a large new rabbit. A white rabbit with floppy ears and pink eyes and a wiffly nose.

"Yours," said Aunt Al.

"Yikes!" said Sophie.

Al Beano, thought Sophie. Funny name.

SLOW AND STEADY
WINS THE RACE

Sophie came up with a name for her rabbit quite simply.

"Why has he got pink eyes?" she asked Aunt Al.

"Because he's albino."

Al Beano, thought Sophie. Funny name, but if you take off the Al — after all, we've got one of those in the family — that just leaves Beano. I like that.

At first, Sophie was worried about Tomboy. What would she think of Beano? Cats killed little, wild rabbits, she felt sure. What about big, tame ones?

She found out the answer very soon after

Beano's arrival, when he was hopping around the floor and Tomboy suddenly came in through the hole in the back of the shed. Sophie had looked around to see the black cat creeping forward, tail lashing. But before she could move, the big white rabbit first gave an almighty thump on the floor with his hind legs and then, with a kind of growl, made a dash at Tomboy, who turned and fled.

Matthew and Mark did not share Sophie's feeling for animals. They were polite to Tomboy and to the new rabbit, but what they were crazy about was sports. Their ambition was to play professional football (on the same team, of course, and in the First Division, naturally) when they were grown-up.

The highlight of the spring term for them was field day. Fast runners both, they were set on beating all the other boys of their age when the great day came.

*The big white rabbit gave an
almighty thump on the floor.*

Sophie was not a fast runner.

"But I would like to win something," she said to Beano as he lolloped around the floor of the potting shed, while she cleaned out his hutch.

Sophie spread fresh sawdust on the floor of the hutch and filled the hayrack, the feeding dish, and the water bottle. "There you are, my dear," she said. "All nice and tidy. In you go, there's a good boy."

She used this last word with confidence. Admittedly, she'd been slightly wrong about Tom, and later about Molly, Holly, and Polly, but Aunt Al had assured her that the pet shop owner had assured *her* that the rabbit was definitely a boy.

She latched the door of the hutch and went to find her brothers.

They were practicing handing off the baton on the lawn, preparing for the junior boys' relay race.

"When it's field day," she said to them, "what could I win?"

"How fast are you?" they said.

"Not very," said Sophie.

"Let's see," said Matthew.

"We'll give you a good start," said Mark.

"From the path here . . ."

". . . to the other end of the lawn."

"Ready?" said Matthew.

"Steady?" said Mark.

"Go!" they shouted.

Sophie plodded off at her best speed, shoulders hunched, arms pumping, a look of grim determination on her face, and when she was halfway across, the boys gave chase. They flashed past and stood waiting for her at the other end.

"You're not," said Mark.

"Not what?"

"Very fast," said Matthew.

*The twins seemed to go almost as fast
when tied together, as separately.*

They looked at one another thoughtfully.

"I know!" said Mark.

"I know what you're going to say!" said Matthew.

"The three-legged race!" they cried.

"What's that?"

"Well, you have a partner . . ."

". . . and you stand next to him . . ."

". . . with your inside legs tied together . . ."

". . . so there's two legs on the outside and one in the middle."

"We'll show you," they said, and they ran off and came back with a piece of old rope.

Sophie watched them. They were so well balanced they seemed to go almost as fast when tied together as separately.

"You want to pick someone exactly your size," said Matthew.

"No good being partners with someone who has really long legs," said Mark.

Sophie sat on a bench, rubbing the end of her nose.

"Exactly my size . . ." she said slowly.

So it was, that at every recess from then on, Sophie and Andrew solemnly practiced for the three-legged race.

At first they fell down a great deal, but then, because Sophie was determined they should succeed, they gradually improved, always remembering to start with the outside feet, and becoming used to a comfortable pattern of stride.

Matthew and Mark even took time off from their training to come and have a look at Sophie and Andrew in double harness.

"Not bad!" they said.

"Good balance."

"Nice rhythm."

"Steady pace."

"They'll be hard to beat!"

Sophie woke up on the morning of field day feeling quite confident that victory would be hers (and Andrew's of course). No other pair could hold a candle to them, she was sure.

To cap it all off, it was a lovely day, sunny and warm, and Sophie went happily to school. She did not worry that there was no sign of Andrew. He's late, she thought. But then when the teacher called his name during attendance, there was no answer!

The secretary put her head around the classroom door.

"Andrew's mother has just called," she said. "He's got the mumps."

"There's always the egg-and-spoon race," the twins said when Sophie told them the terrible news at recess.

"I'm not fast enough."

"You don't have to be fast for the egg-and-spoon," said Mark. "You just have to concentrate on the potato."

"What potato?"

"They don't actually use eggs," said Matthew. "And the fast ones always drop their potatoes."

"Just go steady," they said.

Nobody was surprised that afternoon when, between them, the twins won all the junior boys' races. Matthew just beat Mark in the sixty meters and Mark just beat Matthew in the hundred meters, and, thanks to the pair of them, their team easily won the relay.

Sophie had no such luck in her races. She tried hard despite her disappointment over Andrew, but was usually among the last to finish. Worse, however, was to come.

"Now then," said the teacher who was organizing the three-legged race, "everybody stand beside their partners." And she went around tying legs together.

"Sophie," she said at last, "where's your partner?"

"He's got the mumps," said Sophie in a voice of deepest gloom.

"Then we must find you another. Now, who still hasn't got someone to run with?"

"Me," said a voice. "Samantha's gone on vacation."

It was Dawn.

"Yuck!" said Sophie. "I don't want to run with her."

"Don't be silly, Sophie. Come here, Dawn."

When all the pairs were lined up for the race, it was only too plain that one was dreadfully unsuited. Lanky Dawn with her neat blonde ringlets towered over dark, stocky Sophie, who

When all the pairs were lined up, it was
plain that one was dreadfully unsuited.

looked, as always, as though she had just come through a hedge backward. And it was very apparent that only the length of material binding them together stopped them from putting as much distance as possible between one another.

"Go!" shouted the teacher, and away went the other couples, their arms around each other's shoulders.

Now, all those minutes, hours even, of pain-staking practice with poor, fat-necked Andrew were worth nothing. Sophie led off with her right foot and Dawn did the same, and they fell in a heap.

Struggling up, they stumbled and shambled behind — off balance, out of step, and hope-lessly ill-matched. Time and again they fell, until at last Dawn burst into tears and lay, howling.

Sophie did not approve of crying. She was

"You wimp!" Sophie said, bitterly.
"I ought to thump you."

simply very angry.

"You wimp!" she said bitterly. "I ought to thump you. You're silly, stupid, and sickening, you are," and she undid the binding, got to her feet, and stomped off.

"Tough luck, Sophie," said Matthew.

"It was that crummy Dawn," said Mark.

"There's still the egg-and-spoon race," said Matthew.

"Concentrate on the potato," said Mark.

"You can do it!" they said.

The potatoes were of all shapes and sizes, and by sheer good luck Sophie was given a nice heavy one that fitted well into the bowl of the spoon. That was a help, no doubt about it, but more important was the fact that Sophie remembered her brothers' advice to go steady.

Several of the kids galloped away at the start of the race, especially the still-sniveling Dawn, who was anxious to get as far away from Sophie as she could. And before long potatoes were rolling everywhere on the grass.

Soon all the faster runners were in trouble. The race, it was plain, was between Sophie and Duncan — who was also going along very steadily, possibly because his short legs would carry him no faster.

Neck and neck they plodded on, while the twins yelled encouragement to their sister, and then Duncan tripped and fell, and Sophie came home the winner.

That evening Sophie was sitting in the potting shed, chatting to Beano as he polished off a carrot, when Tomboy appeared in the doorway. Having made sure that the rabbit was safely shut in his hutch, she came over to be stroked and petted.

"Shall I tell you something, Tomboy?" said

Sophie. "Today I won the egg-and-spoon race."

"Yee-oo?" said Tomboy.

"Yes, me. What do you think of that, my dear?" said Sophie.

Her black cat purred very loudly indeed.

*The twins were always rushing everywhere
and shouting at each other.*

LOST AND FOUND

Shortly after field day, Matthew and Mark went to the seashore on a school trip. Sophie was too young to go. Not that she minded — she was fond of the twins, of course, but they were so noisy, always rushing everywhere and shouting at each other, that it would be nice to have a bit of peace and quiet for one week out of the fifty-two. Besides, she had Tomboy and Beano for company.

"Poor Sophie, she'll be lonely," said her mother.

"She'll miss the boys, I expect," said her father.

"Perhaps," said her mother, "we ought to give her a special treat, to make up for not being able to go on the trip?"

"Good idea," said her father, "but what?" They thought for a minute.

"I know!" said Sophie's father.

"I know what you're going to say!" said Sophie's mother, and then they grinned at one another.

"We sound just like the twins!" they said.

Hanging on Sophie's bedroom walls were four pictures, all drawn by Sophie's mother. One was of a cow called Blossom, one was of two hens named April and May, the third was of a Shetland pony called Shorty, and the fourth was of a spotty pig by the name of Measles. These were the animals that would one day belong to Sophie when she was a grown-up lady farmer.

That evening, when her parents came in to say good night to her, Sophie was sitting up in bed, underneath her portrait gallery, looking at a picture book. It was, of course, about a farm. On its cover was a picture of a rather fat farmer and a surprised-looking cow. Instead of sitting on a stool and milking the cow into a pail, the farmer was sitting on the pail and milking her into the upturned stool.

"Look what he's doing!" Sophie's father said, pointing.

"He's forgettable," said Sophie.

"Don't you mean 'forgetful'?" said her mother.

"I've forgotten," said Sophie.

"Well, just remember," her father said, "when you're grown-up and milking your cows, not to be as absentminded as that."

"I shall have a milking machine," said Sophie.

"What, for just one cow?"

"I shall have lots of cows. Blossom will have lots of calves, and then they'll grow up and have calves of their own, and soon I'll have hundreds."

"How would you like to see hundreds of cows?" her mother said.

"All different breeds," said her father.

"And masses of pigs."

"And loads of sheep."

"And horses and ponies."

"And hens and ducks and geese."

"And rabbits?" said Sophie.

"Yes, probably."

"And cats?"

"No. No cats. But every kind of farm animal you can think of, as well as tractors and all sorts of machines. At the Royal Wessex Agricultural Show. Tomorrow. Would you like to go?"

"Yikes!" shouted Sophie. "I won't sleep a

wink!"

"Oh, yes you will," they said. "You have a good night's rest. Sleep tight and don't let the bedbugs bite."

They tucked her in, kissed her good night, and turned off the light. Sophie lay wide awake for what seemed to her like ages. I will never get to sleep, she said to herself after about ten minutes — I'm so excited about tomorrow.

She began to count sheep jumping through a hole in a hedge. At the fifteenth sheep she gave a tremendous yawn, and at the twenty-seventh her eyes closed. Next thing she knew, it was broad daylight.

Sophie sat up and looked at her bedside clock. The little hand pointed to six, the big hand to eight.

"Half past eight!" she cried. "Mommy and Dad must have overslept. We'll all be late getting to the Agricultural Show!"

"Wakey, wakey! Rise and shine!" said Sophie.

She leapt out of bed and ran to her parents' bedroom. Yes, there they were — sleeping soundly!

"Wakey, wakey! Rise and shine!" said Sophie.

They raised bleary faces, and Sophie's father peered at his watch.

"What sort of time do you call this?" he mumbled.

"Half past eight."

Sophie's father sighed.

"It's the little hand that points to the hour," he said, "and the big hand to the minutes. It's twenty to six."

About five hours later (it seemed to Sophie like five years), they arrived at the Royal Wessex Agricultural Society's show ground. Never in her life had Sophie seen so many people — people of all ages, from very old ones being pushed around in wheelchairs to very young ones being pushed around in carriages.

"We'll never see any of the animals with all that crowd," she said.

"Oh yes, we will," her mother said. "But don't go wandering off, Sophie. You stay with us."

"We don't want you getting lost," her father said. "Now, then, where shall we start? Cattle? Pigs? Sheep?"

"Hot dogs," said Sophie.

"But you've just had breakfast."

"I'm starving."

"It's a very warm day for eating hot dogs."

"Not if you have ice cream after," said Sophie.

In the dairy-cattle lines they found Friesians and Ayrshires and Shorthorns and Guernseys and beautiful little doe-eyed Jersey cows, one of which, Sophie said, was exactly what Blossom

"Where shall we start?" asked Sophie's father.
"Hot dogs," said Sophie.

would be like, one day.

Among all the hens in the poultry tent there were two sitting side by side — the spitting images of April and May. And as they walked toward the pig lines, along came a girl leading a Shetland pony that was Shorty to the life. All I've got to do now, thought Sophie, is to see a pig just like Measles. But there was such a crowd of people in the pig lines, almost all of them much taller and wider than Sophie, that she had a job to spot a single pig, let alone a spotty one.

After a bit, she managed to catch a glimpse of some pinky-white ones, and some black ones, and even some red ones with very long snouts, but nothing that looked remotely like Measles.

Sophie, though small, was very determined, and she was not going to give up easily. One minute she was walking along behind her mother and father, and the next, catching sight of a white pig with a dark spot on it, she turned and began to burrow her way through the crowd to get closer to its pen.

But when at last she reached it, she was disappointed to see that it only had two or three spots. She wriggled her way along to the next pen, and the next, but the pigs in these again only had a few spots.

The fourth pen was different. Not that the animal in it was any spottier, but there was a sign above it, which Sophie could not read, and in the pen, brushing the pig's bristly back, was a man.

Sophie decided to consult him. She knew that children should not speak to strange men, but she badly needed this one's help, and anyway he looked like a nice, kind man. He was fat, with a pink face and a squashy nose and rather big ears. In fact, he looked a good deal like the pig that he was grooming.

"Excuse me," Sophie said. "Could you tell me what this sign says?"

The pig man stopped his brushing and looked up.

"It do say 'Gloucester Old Spots,' young lady," he replied. "That's the name of the breed, see?"

"Oh," said Sophie. "They don't have many spots, do they?"

"Not nowadays," said the pig man. "Isn't the fashion no more. Time was, thisyer breed was covered in spots."

"Like someone with measles, you mean?" Sophie said.

The pig man made a deep grunting noise, which, since he was smiling, Sophie took to be a laugh.

"You interested in pigs then, are you, young lady?" he said.

"Yes," said Sophie. "I'm going to be a lady farmer when I grow up."

"Oh ar. And you fancies a pig with a lot of spots on, do you?"

"Yes."

"Well, you might be lucky. Some piglets is born with plenty, now and again."

"Thanks," said Sophie. "Good-bye."

"Cheerio," said the pig man.

He looked over Sophie's head and said, "I reckon she'll make a proper farmer, your little girl will."

Sophie turned around to see a perfectly strange man and woman standing behind her.

"That child has nothing to do with us," the man said.

"Disgraceful," the woman said, "the way some people let little children wander around on their own," and they walked away.

"Well, I never!" said the pig man. "Lost your

"Well, I never!" said the pig man. "Lost your mom
and dad in the crowd, have you, young lady?"

mom and dad in the crowd, have you, young lady?"

Sophie nodded. How will I ever find them again? she thought. Many children would have started to cry, but Sophie did not approve of crying.

"Don't you fret," said the pig man. "I'll tell you what to do. See that tent over there with a flag flying over it?"

Sophie nodded again.

"That's the secretary's tent, that is. You go straight there and tell 'em your name, and they'll say it over the loudspeaker. I'd come with you myself but I can't leave thisyer sow, we'm due in the show ring in a couple of minutes."

Sophie plodded off toward the secretary's tent, and when she was halfway there she heard the blare of a loudspeaker.

"Here is an announcement," said a voice.

"Will a little girl named Sophie come to the secretary's tent, where her parents are waiting for her?"

"Well, I'm coming, aren't I?" said Sophie crossly, and then she saw her mother and father standing outside the tent, looking around anxiously. When they caught sight of her, they ran to meet her.

"Oh, darling!" her mother cried as she grabbed Sophie and hugged her. "We've been worried stiff!"

"Where on earth did you get to?" her father said.

"I was just having a conservation," Sophie said.

"A conservation?"

"With a nice pig man."

"Don't you mean a 'conversation'?"

"That's what I said. We were talking."

"What about?"

"Pigs, of course. Can I have another hot dog?"

"Oh, Sophie!" they said.

"And more ice cream."

Sophie was walking Beano
around the lawn on a leash.

"MUCH TOO YOUNG"

Sophie was walking Beano around the lawn on a leash.

At one time, before the arrival of the rabbit, she had had the idea of treating Tomboy in a similar fashion. After all, people took their dogs for walks — why not their cats? So she had opened her piggy bank and used some of the precious Farm Munny to buy a little collar and leash.

Tomboy had submitted to the fitting of the collar, but when Sophie attached the leash to it and said, "Come on, Tomboy! Walkies!" the black cat had simply lain on her back and batted at the leash with her forepaws like a kitten playing with a piece of string. Tugging, Sophie found, only produced growls and tail-lashings, so she gave up the attempt at cat-walking. She had left the collar on because she thought it looked nice — it was a blue one — until Aunt Al had told her that it was dangerous for an outdoor cat to wear a collar.

"It might get caught on a twig when Tomboy was tree-climbing, you see," she had said, "and then she'd choke herself."

So Sophie had hung up collar and leash in the potting shed until the time that she would be allowed to have a puppy of her own, something that she was hopeful would happen one day.

In the meantime, Beano had arrived, and one morning Sophie tried the blue collar on him. It fitted perfectly — it looked rather nice against his snowy fur and he did not seem to object. "And," said Sophie, "one thing's certain — you won't be climbing any trees." So she left it around his neck.

Beano's hutch was positioned low down, merely raised above the floor of the shed by the height of the four bricks it stood on. This had been done partly because Sophie was not tall, but chiefly so that the rabbit could hop out and down when Sophie was cleaning the hutch, and then hop up and back in again easily. The potting shed door was of course kept shut at these times. Watching him lolloping about on the floor in his new blue collar, Sophie suddenly thought how much he might enjoy a walk on the grass.

She clipped the leash onto the collar and opened the door of the shed. For a few moments Beano sat in the doorway, wiffling his nose madly at all the scents of the garden, and then he hopped out, Sophie following.

She soon found that though you may take a dog for a walk, going wherever you wish, that's

not the case with a rabbit. The rabbit takes you for the walk and goes wherever it pleases.

But there was no doubt that Beano was greatly enjoying this new experience. He hopped around all over the lawn, sometimes so

quickly that Sophie had to run to keep up, and now and again he gave a little buck-jump of excitement. At first he went entirely where he pleased — into the flower beds and then into the vegetable patch — until Sophie hit upon a way, if not to lead him, at least to steer him roughly in the direction she wanted. On their next outing she held the leash in one hand and in the other a Special Rabbit Controller, which she had invented. This was a flat square of strong cardboard which she had fixed onto the end of a bamboo cane, and by holding it, for example, on the left side of Beano's face, she forced him to turn right. She had gotten the idea from remembering how the pig men at the Royal Wessex Agricultural Show had driven their charges to and from the show ring by using screens to direct them. (Her nice pig man had, to her delight, won the breed championship with his Gloucester Old Spots sow.) Now, using the Special Rabbit Controller, she could steer the rabbit away from her mother's dahlias or her father's cabbages, and could guide him back into the potting shed at the end of the outing.

Each day (for by now the summer holidays had arrived) Beano took Sophie for a walk on the grass.

One morning Sophie's father sat on the swing seat by the edge of the lawn reading the Sunday papers and watching Sophie controlling her rabbit (with difficulty, for Beano was in a stubborn mood).

"What you need, Sophie," he said, "is a

Labor-Saving Device."

"What's that mean?"

"I'll show you," her father said. "I have an idea that will take all the hard work out of rabbit-exercising."

He got up and went to his workshop at the back of the garage, and came back in a little while with a hammer and a long iron spike, which he drove into the lawn.

"Now then," he said, "drop the loop on the end of the leash over the spike, and then Beano can go around and around, so far and no farther, and get his exercise and his grazing, and you can put your feet up."

"Daddy," said Sophie, "you're brilliant."

She sat beside him on the swing seat and watched Beano, now safely tethered, nibbling happily away in the sunshine, and presently Tomboy came stalking across the lawn, keeping carefully out of the range of the rabbit,

"Daddy, when can I have a puppy?"

and jumped up on her lap, purring fit to bust.

My own black cat and my own white rabbit, thought Sophie. Who could ask for anything more?

"Daddy?" she said. "When can I have a puppy?"

"Not till you're old enough."

"I'm six this Christmas." (Sophie's birthday was on Christmas Day.)

"Much too young."

"Seven?"

"No."

"Eight then?"

"Possibly."

Sophie rubbed the tip of her nose.

"Matthew and Mark are eight," she said.

"So?"

"So they're old enough to have a puppy.

Only of course they'll need two — one each."

Her father laid down his newspaper.

"I can read you like a book, madam," he said. "You know the twins aren't all that interested in animals, so if they were allowed a puppy (and you can forget about two, right now), you'd take it over. That was what you were thinking, wasn't it?"

Sophie did not approve of telling lies, so she said, "Yes."

"You've got your own black cat and your own rabbit."

"Yes."

"Well then."

Sophie sat silent on the swing seat for a little while, her father rocked it gently with one foot as he read his paper, Tomboy purred, and Beano grazed.

Then she said, "Andrew's only five like me and he's got three dogs."

"Andrew?"

"Yes. You know. Where I fell in the cowpat."

"Oh, the farmer's son."

"Yes. He's got three."

"Imagine."

"Two sheepdogs and a terrier called Lucy."

"But they aren't his dogs, are they? They're his father's dogs."

"Yes. But he's lucky, Andrew is, all the same."

There was another silence, broken only by the purr of the cat and a little squeaking noise as the seat swung to and fro.

"Isn't he?" said Sophie.

"Isn't who what?"

"Andrew. Lucky."

"Mm."

Silence again for a moment. Tomboy jumped down and walked away. Beano sat up and scratched his ear. The seat squeaked.

"She's going to have babies, sometime later on this year, Andrew told me," said Sophie.

"Who is?"

"Lucy."

Sophie's father sighed and folded his newspaper.

"Sophie love," he said, "I've read the same sentence about five times. How about going and asking Mom if she'd put the kettle on? I wouldn't mind a mug of coffee."

And I wouldn't mind one of Lucy's puppies when she has them, thought Sophie as she plodded off. It's not fair. Imagine having to wait till I'm eight. That's nearly two and a half years. And then they'll probably still say "No." I wish I was grown-up.

"Mom," she said, when she had given the message. "When you were a child, did you have a dog of your very own?"

"Yes, I did, Sophie. When Grandpa and

Granny thought I was responsible enough to look after it properly — to feed it and groom it and train it and exercise it. 'You shall have a puppy of your own,' they said, 'once you're old enough.'"

"And how old was that?"

"Twelve."

That evening, when the children were all in bed, Sophie's father said to his wife, "Did you have a dog of your own when you were a child?"

"How odd!" she replied. "Sophie asked me that this morning."

"Really?"

"Yes, and I told her I did, but not till I was twelve. They didn't think I was old enough till then."

"Ah. What sort was it?"

"A little terrier."

"When I was a boy, I always
wanted a little terrier."

"Funny," said Sophie's father. "I wasn't allowed a dog of my own when I was a boy, but I always wanted a little terrier."

"Do you still?"

Sophie's father laughed. "I'm certainly old enough now," he said.

Sophie's mother laughed. "Me too," she said.

*One day the twins came home in
a state of high excitement.*

ONE FINAL PRESENT

Before you could look around, it seemed to Sophie, those sunny summer holidays were over and the children were going back to school.

Matthew and Mark had almost always gone off to play football with their friends, so Sophie had really only seen them at mealtimes.

It was much the same at school, except that now it was proper football with a proper field and goalposts.

One day the twins came home in a state of high excitement.

"What's up with you two?" their mother asked. "Scored a goal each, have you?"

"No, Mom," said Mark. "It's the school plays."

"You know," said Matthew. "At the end of this term."

"We've got parts in the juniors' play!" they said.

"I wish I could be in a play," said Sophie.

"You might be," said Matthew.

"The little kids do one too, you know," said Mark.

"Who do you think we're going to be, Mom?" said Matthew.

"Guess," said Mark.

"I don't even know what the play is," said their mother. "You'll have to tell me that first."

"It's all different bits out of *Alice in Wonderland*," said Mark.

"And *Through the Looking Glass*," said Matthew.

"All put together," they said.

"You're a crazy couple," said their mother. "I would think you're going to be the Mad Hatter and the March Hare."

"No!" they shouted.

"I'm Tweedledum!" said Matthew.

"And I'm Tweedledee!" said Mark.

"And we're going to be all stuffed out with cushions . . ."

". . . to make us look fat . . ."

". . . and have a great battle . . ."

". . . with toy swords!"

"Football and fighting!" said Sophie scornfully when the twins had run whooping away. "That's all boys think about."

"Perhaps you'll get a nice part in your play," her mother said.

The very next day, as it happened, Sophie's teacher said to her class, "Now, after the end of this term, there's a very special day to look

*"Whose birthday do we celebrate
on Christmas Day?" asked the teacher.
"Mine," said Sophie.*

forward to. Who can tell me what it is called?"

A forest of hands shot up.

"Well, Dawn?"

"It's Christmas Day."

"And what's special about Christmas Day? Andrew?"

"You get lots of presents."

"That's not what I meant. Yes, Duncan?"

"You get a lot to eat."

"No, no," said the teacher. "Never mind about presents or food. Christmas Day is special because that's when we celebrate a very important birthday. And whose birthday is that?"

"Mine," said Sophie.

The teacher looked hard at Sophie. Then she opened her attendance book and ran a finger down the class list of dates of birth.

Then she said, "Yes, Sophie, I remember now that your birthday is on Christmas Day.

But I'm talking about a baby who was born nearly two thousand years ago, in Bethlehem."

Dawn's long skinny arm was raised.

"Yes, Dawn?"

"Jesus."

"Yes, that's right. Good girl. Now you all remember the story of Jesus' birth, don't you? He was born in a stable, wasn't He?"

"Yes."

"Why?"

"They were full up in the motel," said Sophie.

"I don't think that's the right word to use, Sophie," said the teacher. "It was simply an inn where travelers rested. But yes, there was no room at the inn, so the baby was born in the stable and laid in a manger. What's a manger, someone? Andrew?"

"It's like a wooden trough," said Andrew. "You put hay in it. But we don't."

110

"Why not?"

"We put feed in it."

"Oh. I see. Anyway, this is what I want to tell you all. At the end of this term we shall have the school concert, and this class is going to act its own little play, all about the birth of Jesus. There'll be Mary and Joseph and the Wise Men and the shepherds and the innkeeper and . . . now who have I forgotten?"

"The ox and the ass," said Sophie. "That could be me and Andrew, couldn't it?"

"No, Sophie, the animals will just be painted on the scenery. Now who will be the most important person in the whole play?"

"Baby Jesus!" they all chorused.

"Please," said Duncan. "Can I be Baby Jesus?"

"He's small enough," said Sophie dryly.

"No, no, Duncan, the baby will be represented by a doll. I couldn't have a live baby on the stage."

"You wouldn't have time," said Sophie.

"It takes nine months, like a cow," said Andrew.

Possibly these last two remarks had something to do with the fact that, when the leading parts in the play were allotted, Sophie and Andrew were passed over.

"Don't worry," said the teacher to those without starring roles. "You'll all be dressing up and singing 'Once in Royal David's City.'"

"I'm in the play," said Sophie that evening.

"Oh, good," said her father. "Who else in your class is in it?"

"Everyone."

"Oh. What's it about?"

"It's an activity play."

"Don't you mean a 'nativity' play?"

"No, it's about Baby Jesus being born."

"Are you Mary?" said Mark.

"No."

"Who is?" said Matthew.

"Dawn," said Sophie.

"Yuck!" they said.

"Well, you can't be Joseph . . ."

". . . or a Wise Man . . ."

". . . or a shepherd . . ."

". . . or the innkeeper . . ."

". . . because they'll all be boys . . ."

". . . so who are you?"

"I'm a crowd," said Sophie.

"Well, at least you won't have any words to learn then," her mother said.

"Except rhubarb, rhubarb, rhubarb," said her father.

"Why rhubarb?"

"That's what everyone says in crowd scenes."

* * *

"That's no good," said Sophie. "It's a girl."

Later, when their class had the first rehearsal of the Christmas play, Sophie and Andrew and the rest of the extras stood at the back of the stage while Joseph and Mary and the innkeeper and the Wise Men and the shepherds were pushed and pulled into their proper places.

Mary, Dawn that is, had brought into school a bald baby doll of her own, and had been preparing to wrap its bare pink body in swaddling clothes beforehand, when Sophie had come by.

"That's no good," she said.

"Why not?" said Dawn.

"Are you blind?" said Sophie. "It's a girl."

But now Mary sat nursing the baby, Joseph standing proudly at her side, and on came the shepherds and the Wise Men bearing their gifts, which they presented. But all the time no one said anything, not a word.

Sophie looked around at all the others in the crowd, but they too were silent. Sillies, she thought, they don't know what to say. But I do, and loudly she cried, "Rhubarb, rhubarb, rhubarb!"

"Anybody would think rhubarb was a rude word," said Sophie afterward to an audience of

two, Tomboy and Beano.

"Nee-o," said Tomboy.

"Well, the teacher got ever so mad with me, and I was only doing what Dad said. She's silly, stupid, and sickening, that's what she is."

Not long after the break, Andrew said to Sophie, "Lucy had puppies."

"How many?" said Sophie.

"Six."

"Yikes!"

"You can come and see them if you like."

Sophie hesitated. She longed to see the puppies, but she knew it would be awful, because she would want one of them so much.

Unwittingly, Andrew made matters worse.

"You could have one when they're old enough," he said.

"No," said Sophie. "They won't let me. Not till I'm eight."

"Well, do you want to see them or not? Make up your mind."

Sophie made it up.

"Okay," she said. "I'd better come over. You ask your mommy to ask my mommy if it's okay."

*   *   *

Sophie never forgot the first time she set eyes on that litter of six fat little terrier puppies. They were two weeks old, their eyes not long opened, and they were just beginning to stumble around on their short legs.

All puppies are delightful creatures, especially to someone who is determined to become a lady farmer.

Lucy, the mother, was a smooth-haired small white terrier with some black patches.

"But the father of the pups," said Andrew's father, "was brown and white, so most of these have some brown on them too. Which one do you like best, Sophie?"

Sophie rubbed the tip of her nose.

"That one," she said, and she pointed to a puppy that was all white except for a black patch over his right eye. "I just wish I could have him."

"Well, I'm going to sell them when they're

"Which one do you like best, Sophie?"
asked Andrew's father.

old enough," said the farmer. "You'd better ask your mom and dad."

"They won't let me," said Sophie. "They say I'm too young."

"And how old are you?"

"I'll be six on Christmas Day."

"Will you, indeed?" said Andrew's father. "Well, they're right. You are too young to have a dog of your own, same as Andrew here. Doesn't your family have a dog at all?"

"No."

"No animals?"

"I've got a cat and a rabbit," Sophie said.

"Ah, well, you aren't doing too badly then. I bet they'll get a dog one day. Come on then, Lucy — in you go with your pups. And Andrew and Sophie — it's time for a snack."

With one last backward look at the white puppy with the black patch over his right eye, Sophie plodded off. I don't want to see them again, she said to herself. If Andrew asks me over before they're all sold, I won't go. I couldn't bear it.

In fact, Andrew did not ask her over again as November and the early part of December sped by, and soon the school plays were upon them.

Sophie's mother and father came with all the other parents to watch.

The nativity play went pretty well, except that one of the Wise Men was silly enough to drop his gift. Sophie, wrapped in a red-checked gingham tablecloth and positioned at the rear of the crowd, remained completely silent, only mouthing "Rhubarb" when she caught her parents' eyes.

As for Tweedledum, he had the most tremendous fight with Tweedledee for stealing his nice new rattle, and, all in all, the plays were a great success.

It seemed to Sophie that it was hardly over

before it was Christmas Eve, the eve of her sixth birthday.

Christmas Day began as usual — the stockings, then breakfast, then the giving out of the presents, all stacked beneath the Christmas tree. Just before they started on that, the phone rang and it was Aunt Al, to wish them the compliments of the season.

When it was Sophie's turn to speak, she said, "How's Ollie?"

"He's fine," said Aunt Al. "He's grown. He's going to be the biggest cat in the Highlands, I should think."

"As big as a Scottish Wild Cat?"

"Shouldn't wonder. Have you had any good presents?"

"We haven't opened them yet."

"Hope you get a nice surprise," said Aunt Al.

As always, the presents were opened one at a

time, youngest first. One for Sophie, then one for Mark, then Matthew, then Mommy, then Dad, and finally a birthday present for Sophie before she began again on her next Christmas one.

But this year, when all the presents had been opened and there was nothing left under the tree, Sophie's father said, "Now everybody stay put and play with your presents. I won't be more than a quarter of an hour," and out he went.

They heard the car start up.

"Where's Dad gone, Mom?" said Matthew.

"To get something."

"What is it?" said Mark.

"One final present."

"Who's it for?" said Sophie.

"All of us."

"For all of us?" said the three children with one voice.

"Yes. It's for Daddy and it's for me and it's for Matthew and it's for Mark and it's for Sophie."

The twins shook their heads.

"I don't get it," said Mark.

"Me neither," said Matthew.

As for Sophie, she suddenly remembered that in all the excitement she had fed neither Tomboy nor Beano, and she went off to give each a special Christmas breakfast.

No sooner was she back in the living room with the others than they all heard the car returning.

"Sit still," their mother said. "Don't move."

The door opened, and in walked their father, carrying something in his arms.

When Sophie saw what is was, for once in her life she did not shout "Yikes!" because her throat had suddenly tightened up so that she could not have gotten the sound out. And

*The door opened, and in walked their father, carrying
something in his arms.*